*Rupert Little Bear Library No. 3*

# RUPERT
## and the
## Enchanted Princess

### MARY TOURTEL

SAMPSON LOW, MARSTON & CO., LTD.
London W.1

Made and printed in Great Britain by Purnell and Sons Ltd.
Paulton (Somerset) and London

# RUPERT AND THE ENCHANTED PRINCESS

IT'S holiday time. Rupert and Bill,
    Each with his butterfly net,
Start out, and some rare specimens
    Both of them hope to get.

"Let's go down to the stepping stones,"
    Said Bill, "for I know there
We're sure to see some lovely ones."
    "All right," said Little Bear.

Down to the stream and o'er the stones
    With happy hearts they went,
Glad to be out that summer morn
    And on their quest intent.

# RUPERT AND THE
# ENCHANTED PRINCESS

ACROSS Rupert's path came flitting then
    A gorgeous butterfly,
They both gave chase. "Oh, look, look, look!
    A Painted Lady," they cry.

Too eager, Rupert missed his aim,
    And lightly fluttered away,
That pretty, dancing butterfly,
    To live another day.

# RUPERT AND THE
# ENCHANTED PRINCESS

JUST then the sound of beating wings
   Quite close to them they heard,
And, turning, swooping down on them
   They saw a great big bird.

They dropped their nets in fright and ran.
   Straight for Rupert that bird came;
Astonished was the Little Bear
   To hear it call his name.

# RUPERT AND THE
# ENCHANTED PRINCESS

THE great bird seized him. Off it flew.
  "Rupert! Rupert!" shouted Bill,
And bade the bird set Rupert down:
  But it flew higher still.

Up, up they rose far in the sky.
  Rupert the bird could hear
Speaking: "Keep calm. I hold you safe,
  And you have naught to fear.

"The King, my Master, whom I serve,
  Bade me go seek for you
And bring you to him. He's a task
  He hopes that you can do."

# RUPERT AND THE
# ENCHANTED PRINCESS

S O swiftly does that great bird fly
    Far o'er land and sea they go.
Till Rupert sees it making straight
    For a Castle down below.

Ere they touched ground at the Castle Gate
    Out ran two men. Cried one:
"Ha! Ha! You've found that Little Bear,
    Good trusty bird. Well done!"

# RUPERT AND THE ENCHANTED PRINCESS

STRAIGHT to the King they went. He stared,
  "Is this Rupert?" asked the King.
"The one to find our lost Princess?
  He's such a little thing."

Then he called him to his side and said:
  "List carefully to me;
My daughter's lost, but when and how
  Is all a mystery.

"Near and far the country has been searched,
  And desolate am I.
Can you succeed where others failed?"
  Said Rupert: "I will try."

# RUPERT AND THE
# ENCHANTED PRINCESS

H E'S given a knapsack packed with food
   And drink; a stick, and so
He's ready. Through the Castle Gate
   The soldiers watch him go.

"To think that little chap," said one,
   "Can find our lost Princess
Where we failed to find a trace! We've seen
   The last of him, I guess."

# RUPERT AND THE
# ENCHANTED PRINCESS

RUPERT wanders through the countryside
    Wishing he had some clue
As to where the Princess really is
    And what were best to do.

He comes soon to an Inn. Thinks he:
    "Many travellers stop here.
Perhaps they've news of the lost Princess."
    Then at the door appear

The host, his son, too; but his tale
    With laughter loud was hailed.
"Do you think," they jeered, "you can succeed
    Where valiant knights have failed?"

# RUPERT AND THE
# ENCHANTED PRINCESS

BY the stables of the Inn he saw
   The house dog and the cat,
Who had overheard what he had asked.
  Said Puss: "I'll tell you that

"One windy night in bright moonlight
   I saw three witches fly,
Bearing one whose dress did gleam with gold;
  'Twas our Princess, thought I."

# RUPERT AND THE
# ENCHANTED PRINCESS

RUPERT walked some way, then stopped
   to rest,
  And turned his head to see
A tiny coach drawn by four mice,
  Whence a small dame looked. Said she:

"Master Rupert, I know whom you seek;
   But far you have to go.
  That Princess as a Golden Flower
   In a garden now doth grow.

"First seek the Lady of the Wood
   In the forest you'll pass through
  Along this road. 'Tis there she dwells:
   She'll tell what next to do."

# RUPERT AND THE
# ENCHANTED PRINCESS

WHEN the little dame had driven off
    Rupert too on his way went
And soon a forest vast he reached,
    Doubtless the one she meant.

How in that forest could he find
    The lady whom he sought
He felt bewildered, there alone:
    "Oh, for some help!" he thought.

"Ha! Ha!" he heard a voice. "I know
    Whom you seek. I'll guide you there."
Rupert turned to see a little man
    Riding upon a Hare

# RUPERT AND THE ENCHANTED PRINCESS

RUPERT followed that strange little man
　　Through winding ways and long
Deep in the forest till they hear
　　Close by a soft, sweet song.

"Hush! 'Tis the Lady of the Wood,"
　　Said he, "you'll find her there
Beyond those rocks." Then off he sped
　　Full gallop on his Hare.

# RUPERT AND THE
# ENCHANTED PRINCESS

A FEW steps farther Rupert sees
     The Lady of the Wood.
"What is your wish?" she asked, as he
     Shyly before her stood.

He told her of his quest. Said she:
     "First you must find a steed
Of spotless white, shod with pure gold,
     To serve you in your need."

# RUPERT AND THE
# ENCHANTED PRINCESS

MANY horses Rupert saw, but not
  The gold-shod one he sought;
Till tired and hungry down he sat.
  'Twas time for lunch, he thought.

His knapsack then he did unsling.
  Roast chicken came to view;
Crisp rolls, some tarts, and also fruit,
  And lemonade there, too.

# RUPERT AND THE
# ENCHANTED PRINCESS

JUST as Rupert started on his meal,
There, trudging down the road,
Came a tinker, with his pots and pans
Making a jingling load.

The tinker stopped and smiled. Said he:
"Why, what a royal spread!
It's long since I have tasted such."
"Please, have some," Rupert said.

# RUPERT AND THE
# ENCHANTED PRINCESS

As they ate together Rupert told
    Of the horse he had to find
With golden shoes. Said the tinker: "Ah,
    Now I recall to mind.

"I've heard of such. But where to look?
    If there is one should know
It's Wayland Smith up in the hills;
    To him you'd better go."

# RUPERT AND THE ENCHANTED PRINCESS

Ended their meal, the tinker said
    When he'd picked up his load:
"You've been so kind, I'll come along
    To set you on your road."

Reaching a stony path, said he:
    "Keep straight on till you view
An anvil. Strike upon it thrice.
    That's all you have to do."

# RUPERT AND THE
# ENCHANTED PRINCESS

RUPERT sees the anvil; a hammer there
 With both his hands he swings:
Three times he strikes, and loud and clear
 The echoing anvil rings.

He hears a voice: "Put down your coins
 And shod your horse will be."
He looks around and looks again,
 But no one can he see.

# RUPERT AND THE
# ENCHANTED PRINCESS

RUPERT heard some steps, and
    Wayland Smith
Came from a cavern near.
   "If you've no horse to shoe," he said,
"Tell me what brings you here."

Rupert explains. "Ah," said the Smith,
   "Little Bear, you're very bold;
For dangerous is the task to get
   That horse with shoes of gold."

"The horse belongs," said Wayland Smith,
   "To Brimbor, an Ogre grim,
Who keeps him in a stable locked,
   And the key it ne'er leaves him."

# RUPERT AND THE ENCHANTED PRINCESS

"**E**ACH day he comes to feed the horse,"
 Said the Smith. "His sight is poor,
So take your chance to slip inside
 When he undoes the door.

"From the stable straight the Ogre goes
 To his dinner, then to sleep,
In his Palace built all underground,
 So, after him you creep

"And wait your chance. When loud he snores
 Go, take the stable key,
That hangs upon a belt he wears,
 Then get the horse and flee."

# RUPERT AND THE ENCHANTED PRINCESS

"NOW keep a brave heart, Little Bear,
    You have not far to go."
Said Wayland Smith, "You can almost see
    From here the place below."

They stood together. Wayland points:
    "Go past those firs. You'll see
Soon after a great riven oak:
    At the stable then you'll be."

Rupert thanked the kindly Smith, who watched
    Him while he was in view
"May you succeed," he called aloud,
    "And good luck go with you."

# RUPERT AND THE
# ENCHANTED PRINCESS

SOON Rupert sees the riven oak,
　　And nearby is a door:
It's the stable of the steed he seeks;
　　Of that he feels quite sure.

A slope there led down to the door.
　　"Here's the place the good Smith meant,"
Thought he, and plucking courage up
　　Towards the door he went.

The door was locked, as Wayland said;
　　But he heard stamp of hoof
And a rattle of a chain within—
　　That a horse was there 'twas proof.

# RUPERT AND THE
# ENCHANTED PRINCESS

THEN he hears the sound of heavy steps.
  It's the Ogre there inside!
A key's thrust in the lock and turned.
  Rupert scarce had time to hide.

In a dark corner close near by,
  When open came the door,
Out stepped the Ogre; then with care
  He locked it as before.

# RUPERT AND THE
# ENCHANTED PRINCESS

SCARCE a moment passed ere Rupert heard
    The Ogre coming back.
To be more free Rupert slipped off
    That cumbersome knapsack.

The Ogre comes with truss of hay,
    Again unlocks the door.
Rupert sees his chance to slip inside,
    Glad the Ogre's sight is poor.

# RUPERT AND THE
# ENCHANTED PRINCESS

**B**UT how he trembled when inside
    And the Ogre turned the key.
Thought he: "I'm fast locked up in here.
    Oh, if he should see me."

Rupert hiding there close by the stall
    Where stood the gold-shod steed,
Watched the Ogre bring some water when
    The horse had had his feed.

At last the Ogre's task is done
    And Rupert sees him go
From the stable by another door
    To his Palace down below.

# RUPERT AND THE ENCHANTED PRINCESS

RUPERT followed down those steps
   That led to a large room brightly lit;
At a table spread with food galore
   He sees the Ogre sit.

Rupert can see a whole roast pig,
   Turkeys and capons fine;
Choice tarts, and fruits, a mighty cheese,
   And flagons of rich wine.

# RUPERT AND THE
# ENCHANTED PRINCESS

RUPERT waited till at last he heard
    Loud snores and then he felt
'Twas now or never to obtain
    The key fixed to his belt.

Now fearfully with timid hand
    To reach the key he tries,
When the Ogre stirs, turns in his sleep,
    And uneasily he sighs.

Rupert dare not move, and scarce dare breathe;
    But how relieved is he
When he sees that he yet soundly slept.
    From the belt he took the key.

# RUPERT AND THE
# ENCHANTED PRINCESS

RUPERT with the key and taking care
    To make no noise then ran
From the Ogre's room and up the steps
    As quickly as he can.

He gains the stable. All is still.
    Rejoiced at his success,
"Oh, horse," said he, "please carry me
    To rescue the Princess."

The moment Rupert spoke those words,
    To Little Bear's dismay,
The white horse with the Golden Shoes
    Gave a loud resounding neigh.

# RUPERT AND THE
# ENCHANTED PRINCESS

"THAT neigh will wake the Ogre up,"
  Thought Rupert in his fear;
And sure enough the shambling steps
  Of the Ogre he can hear.

He hides, as in the Ogre bursts.
  "How now, what made you call?
I fed you well, my horse," he cried.
  "Has aught frightened you at all?"

# RUPERT AND THE
# ENCHANTED PRINCESS

ALL about the Ogre starts to look,
    Uneasy in his mind;
Gropes here, gropes there, peers everywhere;
    But nothing can he find.

Remembering that his sight was poor,
    Rupert, quiet as could be,
Hid in the shadow. "Oh," he thought,
    "If he should miss the key!"

Then Rupert hears retreating steps
    As back the Ogre goes
To his Palace underground again,
    And soon all silent grows.

# RUPERT AND THE
# ENCHANTED PRINCESS

RUPERT ventured from his hiding place.
　　Thought he: "I'll try once more
To get that horse." Scarce had he moved
　　When louder than before

The white steed neighed, and instantly
　　He heard the heavy tread
Of the Ogre coming back again,
　　And quick to hide he sped.

# RUPERT AND THE
# ENCHANTED PRINCESS

"NOW who is here?" the Ogre shouts.
    "His bones for bread I'll grind!"
And groping round he searched and searched:
    Still no one could he find.

Then in anger he turned on the horse.
    "You have deceived me twice,"
He cried, and seizing a big stick
    He struck the poor horse thrice.

# RUPERT AND THE
# ENCHANTED PRINCESS

R UPERT from where he hid had heard
      The sound of Brimbor's blows
Upon the horse. Trembling he waits,
   Till again the Ogre goes.

Straight to the manger Rupert went:
   The horse, still half-afraid,
Turned on him with a frightened glance,
   But this time never neighed.

Rupert spoke to him in gentle tones:
   "Golden Shoes, you've naught to fear
Wayland Smith has sent me for your help,
   And that's why I am here."

# RUPERT AND THE
# ENCHANTED PRINCESS

AND now to mount upon the horse
He climbed the manger there,
When surprised he sees that little man
Who rode upon the Hare.

"Ah, Rupert, I am glad to see
That you have found the steed,"
Said the little man. "Now, be you sure
To follow where I lead;

"For I'll guide you where the Princess is,
Get the saddle, Little Bear;
You'll find it in the harness room.
We've little time to spare."

## RUPERT AND THE
## ENCHANTED PRINCESS

THE little man (a fairy sprite
    He really was, you know)
Had the horse soon saddled, bridled too.
    They're ready now to go.

Golden Shoes steps lightly from his stall;
    And through the stable door
Goes the little man, who points the way
    And gallops on before.

# RUPERT AND THE
# ENCHANTED PRINCESS

THEY'RE safe away. With splendid stride,
    As though glad to be out,
Gallops Golden Shoes. Then suddenly
    They hear an angry shout.

It's the Ogre, furious in his wrath,
    Knowing he'll ne'er regain
The horse whom he had thrashed, and who
    Had warned him twice in vain.

# RUPERT AND THE
# ENCHANTED PRINCESS

O'ER heath and hill, up mountain side
    With speed that ne'er grows less
The white horse carries Little Bear
    To rescue the Princess.

At length they reach a mountain pass
    Said the little man: "Now stay.
Rupert, dismount! From here you must
    Alone go on your way.

"Golden Shoes will stop with me. Meanwhile
    I've directions to give you.
Pay great attention and you'll know
    Exactly what to do."

# RUPERT AND THE ENCHANTED PRINCESS

"NOW, Rupert, listen well," said the little Fairy Man,
   "I'll tell you what you have to do, as clearly as I can.
   Not far off there's a Garden full of flowers rich and rare,
And the lost Princess enchanted as a flower is growing there.
How to find her 'mid the others? Listen, Little Bear so bold:
She's the only one of all there who is formed of purest gold.
But where she is I do not know among those flowers there:
You must search until you find her, hidden in that Garden fair.
Now that Garden e'er is guarded by a Dragon, night and day,
And past him to reach the Princess you must take alone your way.
He's a Dragon somewhat merry. Very fond of riddles he
Will give you three to answer. If you do so you'll be free

To go into the Garden and to seek your lost Princess:
If you fail to answer rightly, he will kill you, nothing less.
But I know what three he'll ask you and the answers here are writ
On this piece of paper. Guard it well for you'll have need of it.
Learn the answers to the riddles: store them in your memory.
When he lets you pass, go boldly. Never mind the Witches three
Whose the Garden is—those Witches who came on a windy night
And stole away the poor Princess, riding through the bright moonlight.
Now these Witches three, their habits and their customs well I know:
Yesterday was Witches' Sabbath to which every week they go.
That means all to-day they're sleeping, and the Dragon knows it too;
Otherwise he'd be more careful and perhaps would follow you.
When you're there and when the Princess in her golden guise you've found
Grasp that Golden Flower quite firmly. Pull it right out of the ground;
And before you'll know what's happened standing radiant there, and free
From the Witches' long enchantment the lost Princess you will see.
You'll both have to dodge the Dragon. From the Garden find some way,
Then come back here, where waiting you, Golden Shoes and I will stay."

# RUPERT AND THE
# ENCHANTED PRINCESS

RUPERT listened carefully to all
   The things he had to do:
Then as he went along he read
   The riddles, answers too.

He learned the answers off by heart,
   But in his mind there's dread
When he sees the Dragon face to face
   They'll all fly from his head.

His way he wends until at length
   By a Gateway he espies
The fearsome Dragon sound asleep
   To his most glad surprise.

# RUPERT AND THE
# ENCHANTED PRINCESS

RUPERT hoped to creep by. Ere he knows
    He's in the Dragon's grip.
"Ha! Ha!" the Dragon said, "young man,
    So you thought by me you'd slip."

"What brings you here?" the Dragon asked,
    And curled his scaly tail
Round Rupert's legs to let him know
    That flight would not avail.

"Oh," Rupert gasped, "I've only come
    Your garden here to see."
Said the Dragon: "Well, I'll let you in
    If you answer riddles three."

44

# RUPERT AND THE
# ENCHANTED PRINCESS

"I'LL try to answer all you ask," said Rupert, Little Bear.
    "We'll see," the Dragon, sneering, said, fixing him with stony
    glare.
How Rupert hopes his memory won't fail him! "Now, the Moon,"
The Dragon cried. "What does it weigh? Be quick and answer soon."
Said Rupert: "Just one hundredweight. I know that is a fact.
Because it has four quarters and that makes the weight exact."

"Now, number two," the Dragon said. "Suppose you looked on high
One cloudless night, how many stars are there in all the sky?"
"Nine million, ninety thousand, nine hundred and then three,"
Said Rupert. "If you think I'm wrong count for yourself and see."
The Dragon paused and scratched his head. "Now," thought he, "by my
    tail!
He's answered two. Now for the third. At that one he must fail,
Or I'll have to keep my promise and let him go inside
The garden. Ha, young clever sir, come tell me this," he cried:
What key won't unlock anything, though of great use it can be?"
Said Rupert: "I am right, I think, if I mention the—donkey."

# RUPERT AND THE
## ENCHANTED PRINCESS

"OH, bother you. You've guessed all three,"
Said the Dragon. "Pass inside:
Lucky for you my mistresses
Sleep all to-day," he cried.

"Don't pick the flowers. Keep to the paths.
You may stay just half an hour."
Little he dreamed that Rupert knew
About the Golden Flower.

# RUPERT AND THE
# ENCHANTED PRINCESS

THROUGH the Gateway little Rupert goes
  To a lovely garden there.
With lawns, pools, avenues of trees,
  And flowers everywhere.

'Mid all the myriad blooms that grew
  In that secluded place
Search as he would Rupert could find
  Of the Golden Flower no trace.

The time grows short, and if he fails
  Such chance won't come again
To find the Princess—all his toil
  And trouble done in vain!

# RUPERT AND THE
# ENCHANTED PRINCESS

ALMOST as he had hopeless grown
   A gleam of gold near by
Shining midst weeds and rubbish there
   At that moment caught his eye.

Oh could that be the Golden Flower?
   He'd not thought to find it there
Growing in that neglected spot
   Midst all that garden fair.

Yes, he could see all gold it was
   And knew that he had found
The Enchanted Flower. He tugged and pulled
   To root it from the ground.

# RUPERT AND THE
# ENCHANTED PRINCESS

UP came the Flower, root and all;
    Then vanished from his hand,
And just exactly where it grew
    He sees the Princess stand.

"How grateful am I, Little Bear,
    That you have set me free
From the witches' spell. How to escape
    From the Garden? Please help me."

# RUPERT AND THE
# ENCHANTED PRINCESS

WHERE the sister Witches sleep one stirs;
    In restless dreams she moans.
Then wakes up; cries: "A stranger's here!
  I feel it in my bones.

"Someone who seeks the Golden Flower."
    But the others, sleepy, say:
"Nonsense, sister, who could come in here
    While the Dragon guards the way?"

# RUPERT AND THE
# ENCHANTED PRINCESS

THE Dragon meanwhile anxious grew:
　　He knew he had done wrong
In letting Rupert go in there.
　　He wished he'd come along.

Thought he: "I must go after him
　　And see what he's about."
He left his Gate just as there came
　　The sister Witches out

Into the garden, roused from sleep.
　　One saw him: "Look," cried she,
"That rascal Dragon's left his gate
　　Unguarded, as you see."

## RUPERT AND THE
## ENCHANTED PRINCESS

IN anger then the Witches call
   The Dragon, who in fear
Came shambling up. "You've let," they said
   "A stranger pass in here."

"Oh no, oh no," the Dragon said,
   As the tears streamed down his face,
For he fears that they will punish him;
   "No stranger's in this place."

## RUPERT AND THE
## ENCHANTED PRINCESS

RUPERT, with the Princess, now herself,
    Sought their stealthy way to where
The Gateway is, hoping by chance
    Thus to escape through there.

Doubtful, the little Princess says:
    "It's hopeless that, I fear;
For the Dragon never leaves his post:
    There's no other way from here.

"Then by the Witches we'll be found."
    "Come," said Rupert, "let us try;
Perhaps the Dragon's gone to sleep,
    And then we can creep by."

# RUPERT AND THE
# ENCHANTED PRINCESS

"OH, Rupert, look," the Princess cried,
    "There are the Witches three,
And the Dragon too." "Come," Rupert said,
    "That's lucky, don't you see?"

"We'll slip away now to the Gate
    While they're all talking thus:
They are so busy—now's our chance—
    And so they won't see us."

## RUPERT AND THE
## ENCHANTED PRINCESS

RUPERT and the Princess make their way
　　As quietly as can be,
Till they have to cross an open space
　　To where the Gate they see.

They dread that last bit, but both run,
　　Hoping they won't be seen:
But a Witch looked round and caught a glimpse
　　Of a dress with golden sheen.

Then loud she yelled: "Look, sisters, look.
　　'Tis the Princess. Haste to get
Our brooms and follow on their track
　　And we will catch them yet."

## RUPERT AND THE
## ENCHANTED PRINCESS

OUT through the Gate and down the road
    Rupert and the Princess ran
To the waiting-place. "Come, mount at once,"
    Called out the little man.

Fast as the wind they gallop on;
    The little man looks back
To see behind them in the sky
    The Witches on their track.

Have they been seen? They are not sure.
    In the valley down below
Lies a forest thick with leafy trees:
    Towards that to hide they go.

# RUPERT AND THE
# ENCHANTED PRINCESS

DEEP in that forest 'mid the trees,
   Hid by their leafy screen,
They hope the Witches pass o'erhead,
   While they remain unseen.

Said the little man: "Wait here. You're safe;
   I'll go ahead and scout.
And ask the squirrels and the birds
   If the Witches are about."

Ere very long he's back. He calls:
   "All clear! They've gone away;
And now to hasten to your home
   Princess, without delay."

# RUPERT AND THE
# ENCHANTED PRINCESS

UPON their way they speed again,
    Though oft their looks they cast
Skyward. No Witches there! They hope
    Of them they've seen the last.

At length o'erjoyed, the Princess sees
    Her home come into view;
But the little man feels sad, for soon
    He must bid them all adieu.

# RUPERT AND THE
# ENCHANTED PRINCESS

THE little man then stopped his Hare.
    Said he: "You're safe at last,
So here I leave you, glad to know
    That every danger's past.

"I go back to my forest home.
    Princess, ride on; for there
The King awaits you. And farewell
    To you also, Little Bear."

"Stay," said the Princess, "stay with us;
    Glad I know the King will be."
He shook his head and waved his hand,
    And swiftly back rode he.

# RUPERT AND THE
# ENCHANTED PRINCESS

STRAIGHT for the Castle then they ride.
  Oh, how the soldiers stare
To see safe back their lost Princess,
  And with her, Little Bear.

"Where's the King, my father?" then she asked.
  "Princess," the soldiers say,
"He mourns for you as lost, and ne'er
  Comes out in light of day."

# RUPERT AND THE
# ENCHANTED PRINCESS

SHE hastened through the Castle doors;
   To her father's room she hied,
Taking Rupert with her. "Father dear.
   "I'm here and safe," she cried.

The old King, who so long had mourned
   His child in grief profound
Could scarce believe that there she stood—
   His daughter, safe and sound.

O'erjoyed he was, and when he saw
   Rupert standing shyly there
"To you I owe this all, he said,
   "My valiant Little Bear."

# RUPERT AND THE ENCHANTED PRINCESS

AND great was the rejoicings to know that not in vain
  Had Rupert ventured forth and brought the Princess home again.
  A noble feast there was indeed; Rupert the honoured guest;
And the King with his own royal hand pinned a medal to his breast.
The Princess, and the King as well, told Rupert he could stay
With them as long as e'er he liked, e'en for ever and a day.

Rupert thanked them; but he said: "Back home at once I'd like to go,
For Mummy, Daddy too, will wonder what has kept me so;
They'll be worried, very anxious, and oh I want to see
Them both again, so send me home if you please, your Majesty."
So the King said: "Fetch that same big bird and tell the Chamberlain
He must take dear little Rupert back." So off he went again,
Carried safely over land and sea exactly as before,
Save that the bird bore him right back to his own cottage door.
Those Witches three, enraged to know the Princess got away,
From venom, wrath, and bitter spite all died the self-same day;
And the Dragon took their garden and keeps it to this hour
Often thinking about Rupert and the little Golden Flower.
The Ogre's locked for ever in his Palace underground
For Wayland Smith made a great chain by which his doors are bound.
And Golden Shoes? The Princess took him for her very own;
And no one rides him save herself: he's kept for her alone.

## THE END